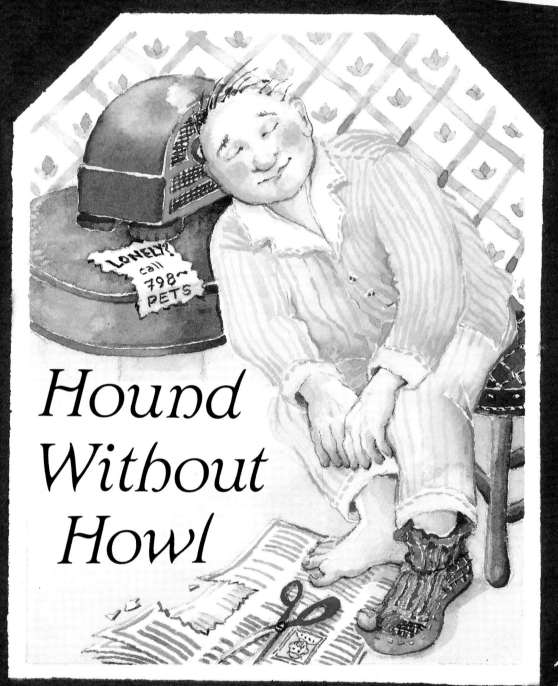

Hound Without Howl

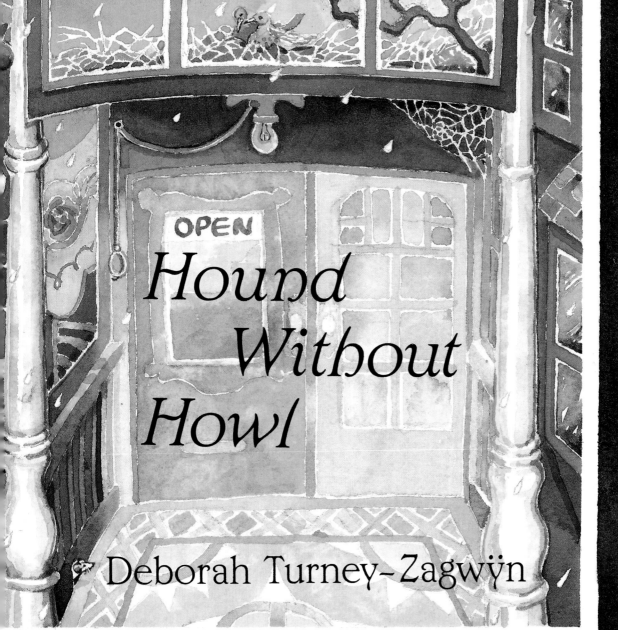

OPEN

Hound Without Howl

Deborah Turney~Zagwÿn

lonely
hear
wel

Howard was a bachelor who loved opera. He hummed off key to the radio but couldn't sing a note. He longed for a musical companion.

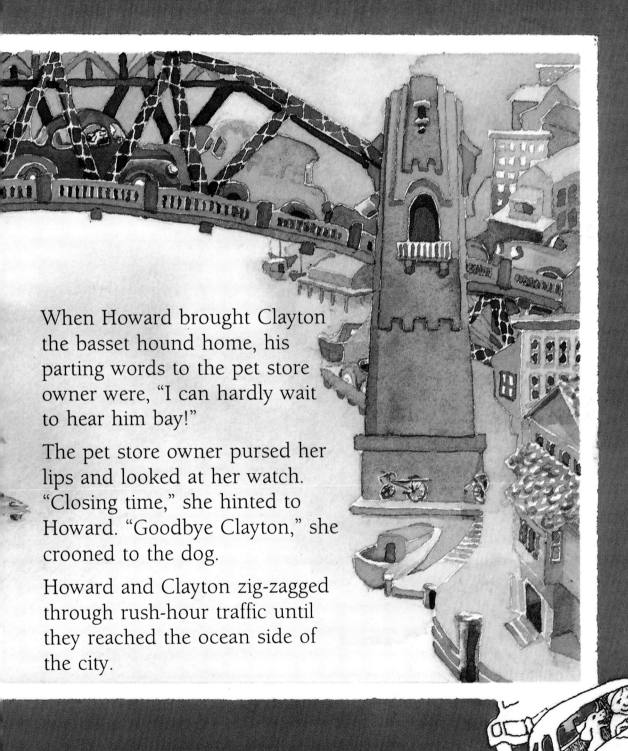

When Howard brought Clayton
the basset hound home, his
parting words to the pet store
owner were, "I can hardly wait
to hear him bay!"

The pet store owner pursed her
lips and looked at her watch.
"Closing time," she hinted to
Howard. "Goodbye Clayton," she
crooned to the dog.

Howard and Clayton zig-zagged
through rush-hour traffic until
they reached the ocean side of
the city.

The little houses clung like buttons to a bevelled bluff threaded together with alleyways and rickrack fences. Howard motored Clayton to a clapboard cottage high above the bay.

Clayton wagged his approval. There was a cozy clapboard doghouse in the front yard. Behind that, a silver dog dish beamed like a spaceship on the step.

figaro figaro

"You might feel inclined to bay,
Clay — on this doorstep,"
Howard coaxed as they stepped
into the house.

"Or here." He pointed at the carpet in front of the pebble-patterned hearth.

"Perhaps this verandah with its veil of ivy and passionflowers will become your favourite spot." Clayton was speechless. Only his wag was working.

Weeks passed. The friendship
between Howard and Clayton
flourished. After breakfasts Clayton
drowsed on the step, his bones
warmed by puddles of early
morning sunlight. Inside, Howard
drank his coffee and read his paper

In the afternoons Clayton sprawled in his doghouse while Howard did yard work.

The hound slept after dinners on the
plush mat below the pebble-patterned
hearth. Howard washed his plates and
polished the dog dish.

In the evenings Clayton sought the verandah, loving its cool veil of ivy and passionflowers.

There, the salty nip of the sea breeze teased his nostrils and the heavy scent of passionflowers lulled him to sleep.

"You are such a relaxing companion," Howard murmured. The dog was too contented to bay.

One evening Howard measured Clayton's doghouse. Clayton, digesting his dinner by the hearth, heard sounds of sawing and hammering. He shuffled out to investigate Howard's handiwork.

"It's a bay window Clayton! Howard hugged the basset. "You may feel a howl coming on soon!"

Clayton's sleep was deep that night. The window gave his doghouse a transparent feeling. He did not wake up to bay.

Next morning Howard was undaunted. He poured half a box of doggy chow into a pot and carried it to the stove. Then he added four cups of water and five bay leaves, winked at his cookbook and waited for the mixture to boil.

Clayton, who was airing his ears and sunning his toenails on the doorstep, picked up the scent. It was the smell of — DOG FOOD SOUP. After it had cooled, Clayton slurped it down. It tasted strongly of bay leaf.

As the hound ate, Howard watched him for baying symptoms. But none occurred.

Howard did not give up easily. To keep Clayton's spirits up, he took him shopping at the Bay. They went to the library to read about the Indian port of Bombay on the Arabian Sea. They lunched at a quaint café and quenched their thirst with iced bayberry tea.

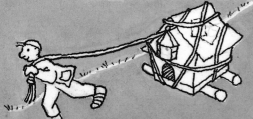

On their return, Howard moved Clayton's doghouse from the front yard to the back yard to give it a bay view.

Nothing worked. Howard had used up all his ideas. It was time he admitted to himself that Clayton was a hound without howl, a mutt without music — a bayless basset.

Howard took Clayton
for a walk one evening
to prove that their friendship could withstand such a
disappointment. After all, they loved
one another. They appreciated the same
things: doorsteps, pebble-patterned hearths, verandahs.
They valued the salty smell of the sea and the
brightness of the stars. It was easier to think and walk
downhill than to think and walk uphill,

so Clayton and Howard
followed the slope downwards
until they could follow it
no further. They had
reached the bay.

It was a wonderful night for considering an almost-perfect friendship. The ocean was very calm. It rocked in and out quietly, slapping ever so gently on the sand.

Clayton padded to the water's edge and let the cool sea brine tickle his tummy and soothe his paws. Howard found a log nearby and gazed up at the sky.

The moon was climbing. It had a familiar shape. It shone like a dog dish. It rose up above the bay and smiled down on them. Clayton whined.

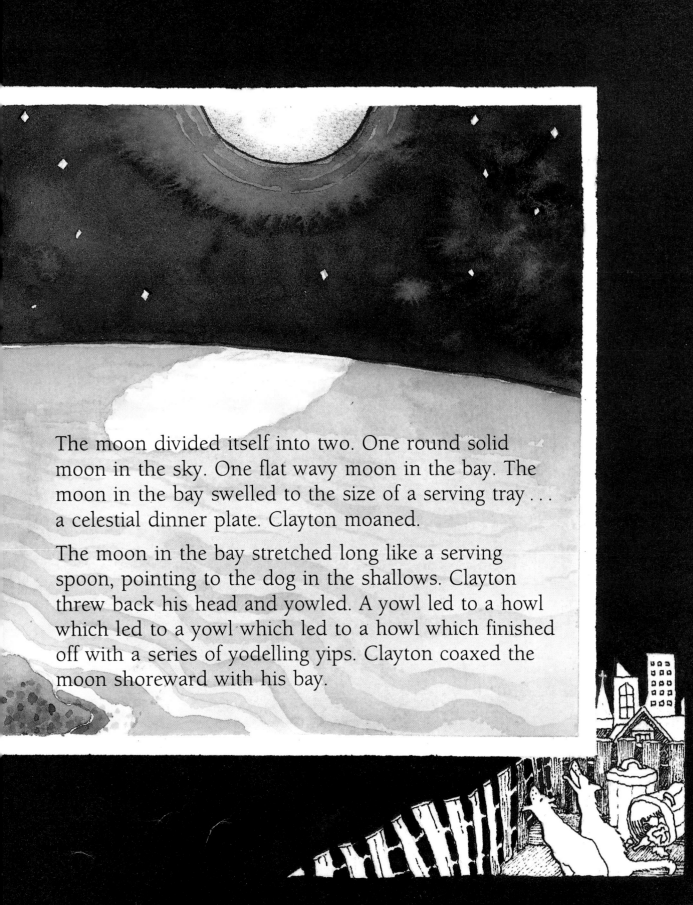

The moon divided itself into two. One round solid moon in the sky. One flat wavy moon in the bay. The moon in the bay swelled to the size of a serving tray . . . a celestial dinner plate. Clayton moaned.

The moon in the bay stretched long like a serving spoon, pointing to the dog in the shallows. Clayton threw back his head and yowled. A yowl led to a howl which led to a yowl which led to a howl which finished off with a series of yodelling yips. Clayton coaxed the moon shoreward with his bay.

Howard stared at the hound with his rear end and front paws soaking up the seawater. Clayton's call was music to his ears.

Howard was a bachelor who loved opera.
Clayton was a dog who sometimes sang.
Theirs was now a perfect friendship.

For Graham, a hound at heart, and Sahara, a true hound!
D.T.Z.

Copyright © 1994 Deborah Turney-Zagwÿn

Publication assistance provided by The Canada Council.

Orca Book Publishers
PO Box 5626, Stn B
Victoria, BC V8R 6S4
Canada

Orca Book Publishers
#3028, 1574 Gulf Road
Point Roberts, WA 98281
USA

Canadian Cataloguing in Publication Data
Zagwyn, Deborah Turney.
Hound without howl
ISBN 1-55143-017-7 (pbk).
 1. Title.
PS8599.A42H6 1994   JC813'.54
C94-910365-9   PZ10.3.Z33Ho 1994
Printed and bound in Hong Kong
Design by Deborah Turney-Zagwÿn
10 9 8 7 6 5 4 3 2 1